Sossy & Juju

Written by
Meenalosini

Illustrated by
Swetha Prakash

Ukiyoto Publishing

All global publishing rights are held by

Ukiyoto Publishing

Published in 2023

Content Copyright © Meenalosini

ISBN 9789360163921

All rights reserved.

No part of this publication may be reproduced, transmitted, or stored in a retrieval system, in any form by any means, electronic, mechanical, photocopying, recording or otherwise, without the prior permission of the publisher.

The moral rights of the author have been asserted.

This is a work of fiction. Names, characters, businesses, places, events, locales, and incidents are either the products of the author's imagination or used in a fictitious manner. Any resemblance to actual persons, living or dead, or actual events is purely coincidental.

This book is sold subject to the condition that it shall not by way of trade or otherwise, be lent, resold, hired out or otherwise circulated, without the publisher's prior consent, in any form of binding or cover other than that in which it is published.

*This title is produced in Association with
Pachyderm Tales*

www.pachydermtales.com

ACKNOWLEDGEMENT

I whole heartedly thank,

   Mohanasundari Jaganathan,

(Managing Director of Sharp Electrodes Pvt Ltd)

for funding this project.

Without her, this book would not be possible!

This book was a part of workshop conducted in our college, NGM College Pollachi and Pachyderm Tales.

I whole heartedly thank our management, our teachers and HOD of English Dept, NGM as well as Suja Mam for this initiative.

Thanks to my friend to support and help me to complete my work.

There were two different types of areas, separated by a river in between them.

There lived a giant creature on one side which had a long nose and teeth. It was 10 feet tall. There were many trees that were smaller than this creature.

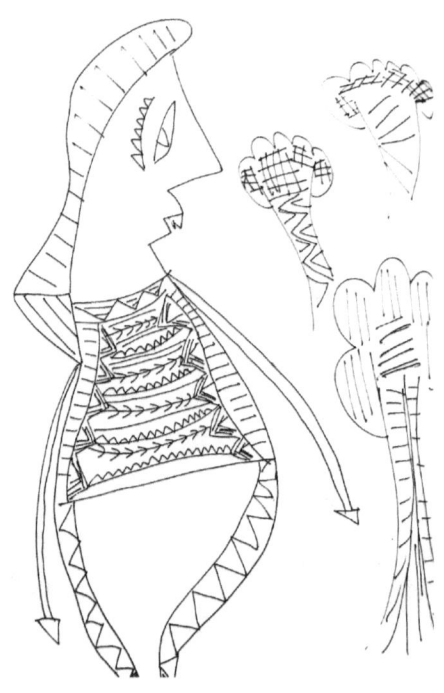

On the other side, there was a clan of many Lilliputians living in the tall tree that goes to the top of the sky and in between the clouds, hovering over both the sides of the river. There are almost hundred families of Lilliputians living in it.

Lilliputians were always very active in doing their work. But they didn't know how to climb trees. They used ladders for their activities.

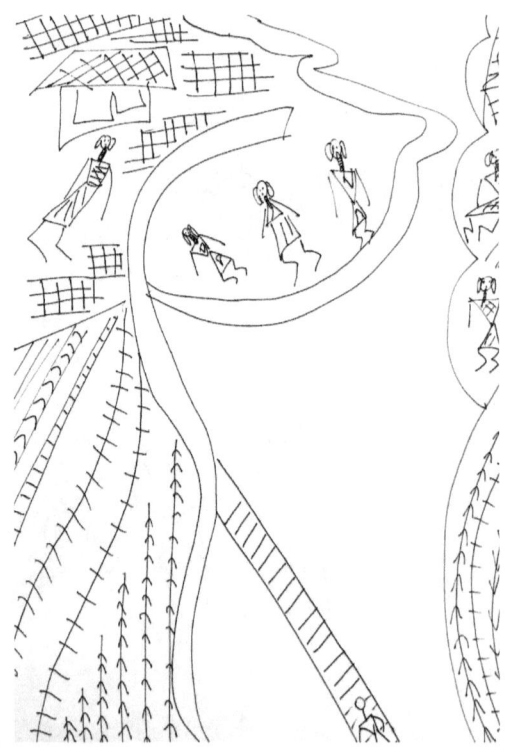

Lilliputians have long ears and a long tongue which flows out of their mouth up to their neck.

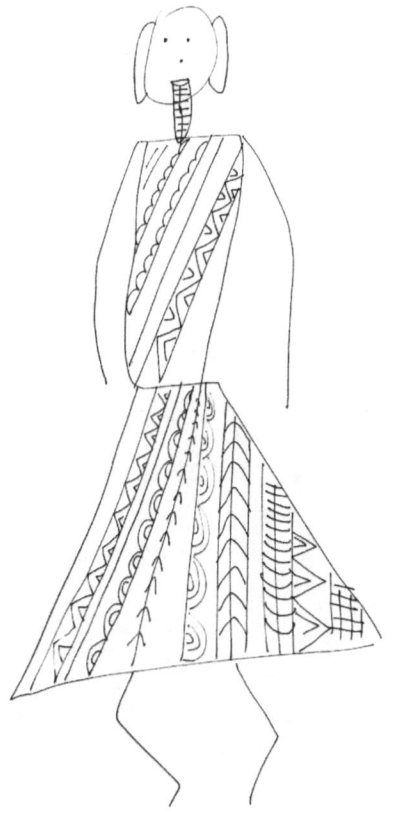

Lilliputians are fond of eating wheat. So, they sowed wheat on their lands.

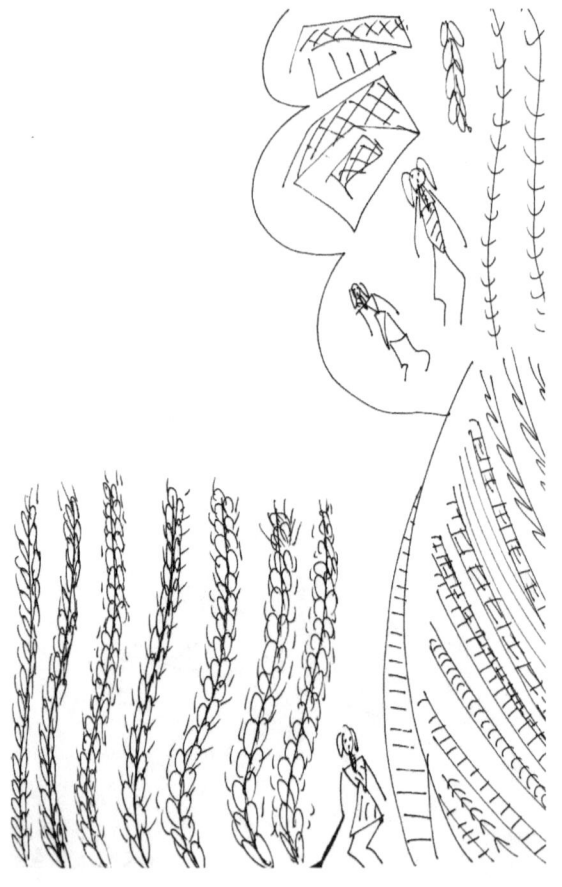

There was a one curious Lilliputian called Soosy.

She was very active and always curious. She asked questions about everything that others do.

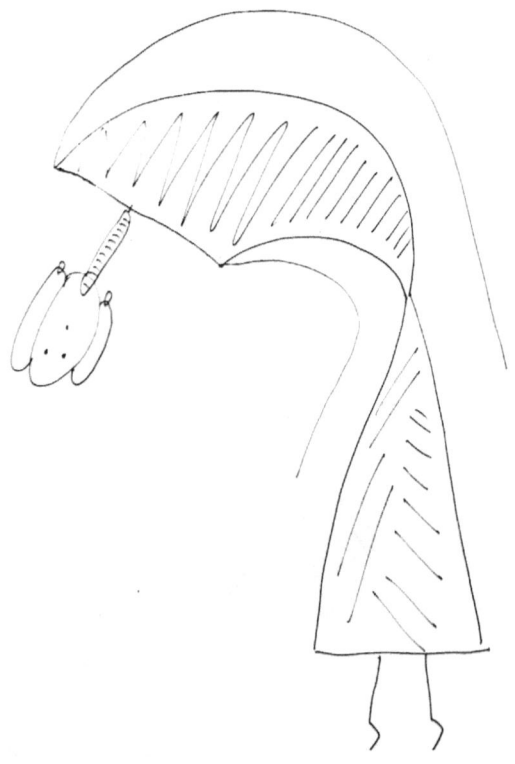

The name of the giant creature who lived on the other side was Juju. He was very lazy. He always sleeps like a log in the afternoons.

Juju usually wanders all over the area at morning times in search of food.

He also watches the activities of the Lilliputians and especially the works of Soosy whenever he has free time.

He feels sad that he couldn't do the activities like Lilliputians because of his big figure.

One day, he watches how Soosy jumps and plays in the river. He wanted to live the life of Soosy.

On the other side, Soosy also watches Juju's work from a distance.

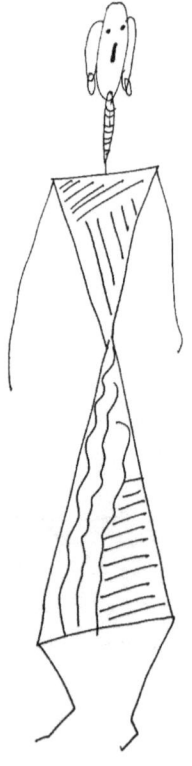

One day, she notices Juju happily tasting the varieties of fruits which was available only from the top of the tree.

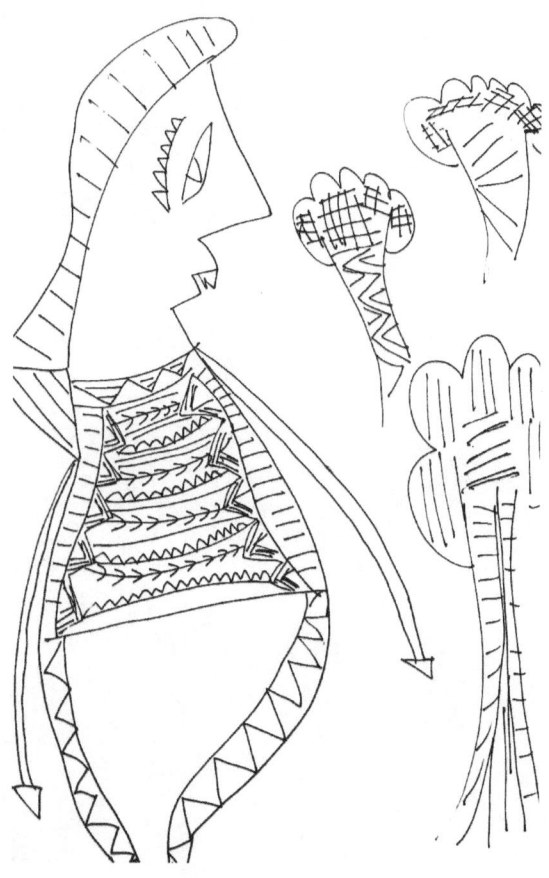

She also wanted to taste the fruits freely, but she feels sad that she didn't know climbing.

She too wished to live the life of Juju so, she can eat the all varieties of fruits.

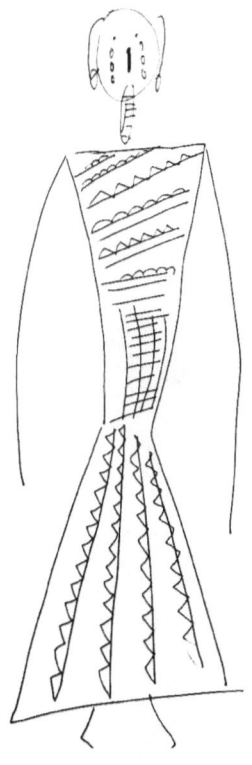

Juju and Soosy wished to exchange their lives without knowing each other.

Both gets a boon from God. Soosy was granted the wish to live Juju's life and Juju was granted the wish to live Soosy's life.

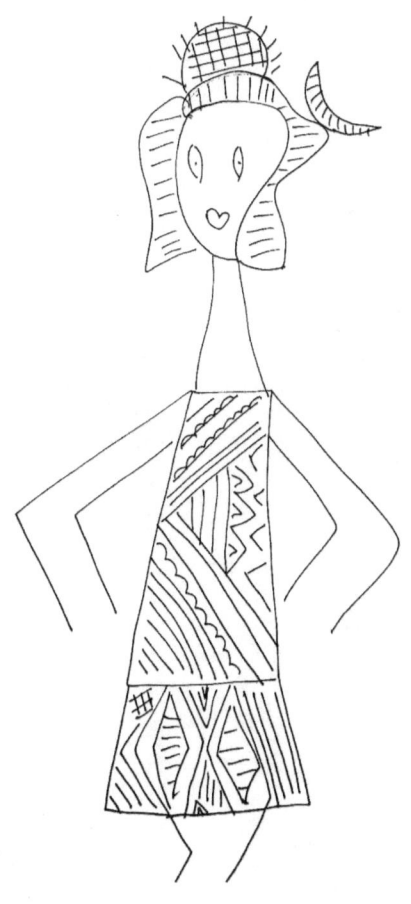

After changing, both were very happy and started enjoying their lives by fulfilling their needs.

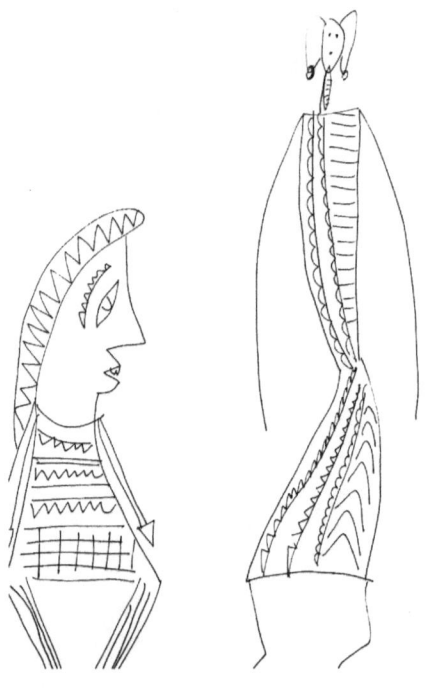

Now, Soosy was a giant creature. She eats and enjoys whatever she wants.

Juju was a Lilliputian, He jumped and played in the river however he wants.

After somedays, Juju felt hard to see trees as he changed in to Lilliputian.

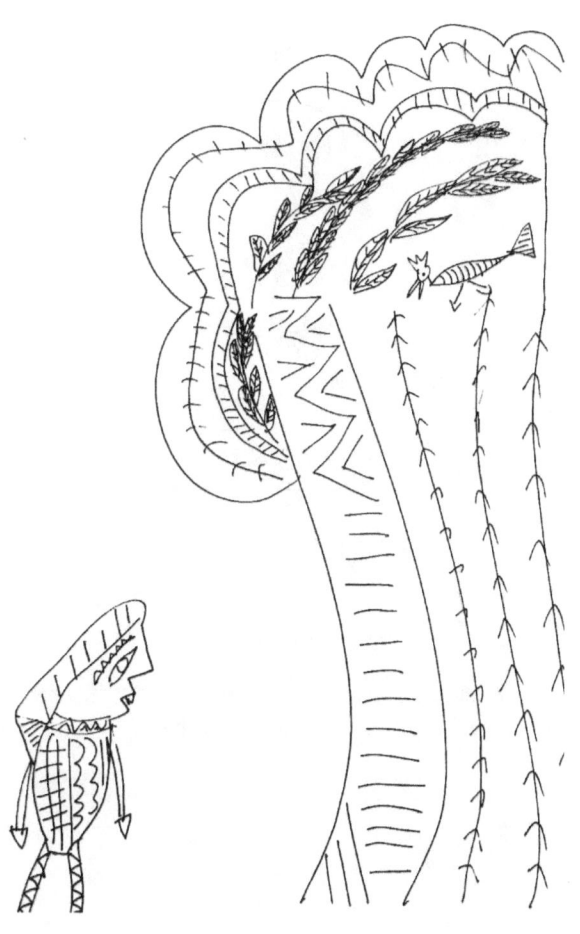

Soosy also felt tough that she can't play in the river as she was a very huge figure now.

Both realized their mistake and asked for forgiveness from God.

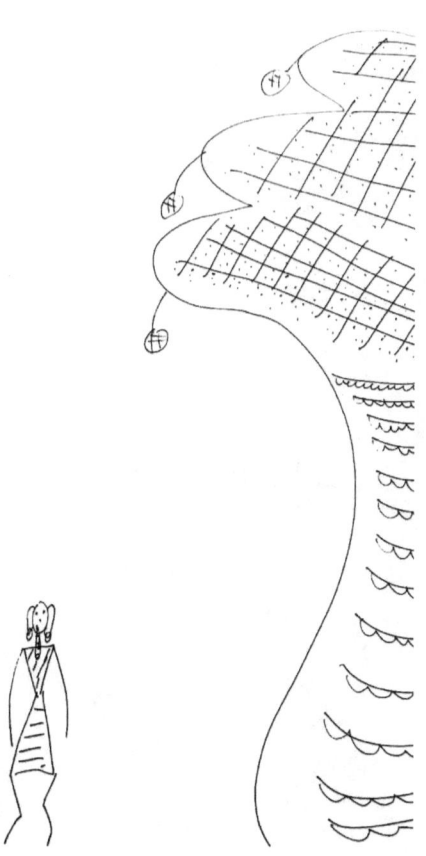

They asked God to change them in to their original forms. Finally, both were happy as they returned to their original forms.

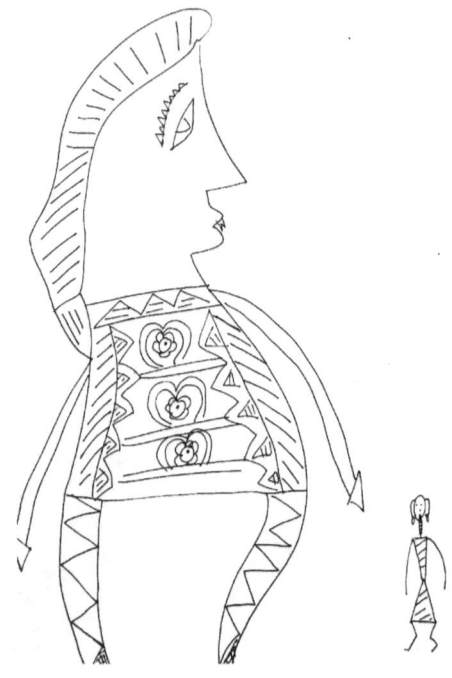

The Author

Meenalosini is currently pursuing under graduation in English Literature. She was brought up listening to many moral stories from her mother. She used to study small stories in her childhood. This habit of reading helped her to learn many things in the form of stories. In her childhood, by the stories, she was influenced by the main characters she read about and she wished to help or to be like the protagonist of the story, which was the inspiration to write her own story! She also discussed the stories which she had read with her family and friends, sharing her thoughts about that story. This helped her to critically analyze each and every situation she pens.

The Illustrator

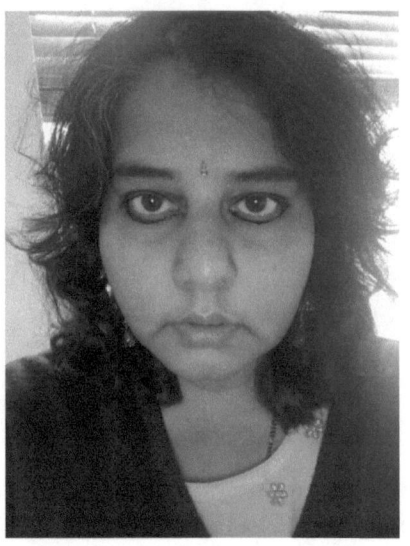

Swetha Prakash has illustrated a few books but none surpass the incredible experience of illustrating this book. Swetha Prakash had trained in Indian folk art illustrations and adds a contemporary touch when working on the picture book genre.

www.ingramcontent.com/pod-product-compliance
Lightning Source LLC
LaVergne TN
LVHW041643070526
838199LV00053B/3532